HOLIN' UP

REAL ESTATE RESCUE COZY MYSTERIES, BOOK 5

PATTI BENNING

SUMMER PRESCOTT BOOKS PUBLISHING

CHAPTER ONE

"And the best part? The raccoon moved out, and I haven't seen him since."

Flora Abner stood in the middle of her newly renovated shed, a bright grin on her face. Violet, one of her closest friends, looked around with an expression that was both amused and a little impressed.

"It *does* look pretty good. I can see why it took you and Grady so long to finish fixing it. It's hardly recognizable."

The shed had been a wreck before Flora and Grady, another close friend and her partner-in-renovation had gotten their hands on it. The roof was leaking, the rafters and loft had been slowly rotting away, parts of the siding were missing, and the shed door had hung crooked and barely closed. It had looked like one good gust of wind could have blown it over.

After weeks of hard work, they had reinforced the supports, replaced the roof and the siding, fixed the rafters and laid down new boards for the loft, and had leveled out the lumpy dirt floor and put down boards for a wooden floor. The entire thing had gotten a fresh coat of paint inside and out, and the single, oversized door had been replaced with two smaller doors that swung easily on quiet hinges.

Most importantly, Flora could now seal the shed up tightly to keep unwanted pests *out*. The raccoon that had plagued her for months was gone. She no longer woke up to see its beady little eyes glowing on the footage from her security cameras, and her garbage was safe from curious little paws again.

"It feels good to finally be finished with this project," Flora said as she walked out of the shed. She paused to shut and bolt the doors behind her, then took a step back to admire the building for a moment.

"What are you going to do next?"

Turning away from the shed, Flora fell into step next to Violet. The two of them walked around her house, through the freshly mowed grass. The flower beds she had extended around the sides of the house were full of fresh blooms, filling the air with a sweet, floral scent.

"Well, we're going to get gravel for the driveway tomorrow," she said. "Grady knows a guy who owns a gravel lot just north of town. I think his name is Connor, and supposedly he gives Grady discounts whenever he buys gravel from him for one of his handyman jobs. So next time you come over, you won't have to watch out for those pot holes."

"Thank goodness," her friend said. "It's one thing for you and Grady, with your trucks, but my poor car always scrapes along the ground whenever I forget to dodge that big one right at the entrance to your driveway."

"I mean, the fact that you still forget after you've been coming over for months is *sort of* on you..."

Violet rolled her eyes as they rounded the front of the house. "Hold on, Grady knows a Connor who owns a gravel lot? Why does that sound familiar?"

"I have no idea why you're asking *me*. Newcomer, remember?"

Her friend snapped her fingers. "I remember. I think his wife went missing a couple of years ago. It was big news around town for a couple of weeks."

"Well, I don't know anything about that. If you're thinking of the right guy, I feel bad for him. That has to be hard."

Their drinks were still on the little table in between the two rocking chairs on the porch. The living room window was open, and Flora could see her fluffy white Persian cat, Amaretto, sitting on the sill behind the screen, gazing out at them with sharp yellow eyes. Amaretto had developed an obsession with the outdoors. It had never been an issue back when Flora lived in an apartment in Chicago, but here, she was constantly fighting the cat back whenever she opened the door.

Unfortunately for Amaretto, she was a house cat through and through. Flora didn't like her chances of surviving on her own in the wilds of Kentucky, so she was meticulous about keeping the cat inside. She was just glad her furry companion hadn't yet figured out that she could claw through the screens.

Wiggling her fingers at Amaretto in a wave, Flora sank into one of the rocking chairs before sipping from her glass of lemonade. She had added raspberries and a sprig of mint leaves — both from her neighbor Beth's garden — to the drink. It felt a little sacrilegious to add such lovely, homegrown treats to a drink she had made from a powder, but she just didn't have the patience to squeeze juice from lemons every time she wanted a fresh pitcher of the stuff.

Violet took the seat next to her and started rocking her chair slowly. It was a slow, peaceful sort of afternoon. Flora had spent the morning tidying up the house, paying her bills, and otherwise catching up on all of the little chores she had let slide over the week. It was a day off for her, which meant she wasn't actively working on any projects. Slowly but surely, the house was coming along. She had a year and a half to flip it and sell it for a profit, and she was becoming more and more certain she would be able to.

The only problem was, the longer she stayed here, the less she wanted to. She liked the slow-paced life she had found here in Warbler. She liked her friends, and she liked the house she was fixing up with her own two hands. Before she moved here, she thought flipping houses for a living sounded

5

great. She could move every two years and constantly experience new areas and meet new people, all while giving run-down homes a second chance at life. She would be her own boss, would make her own schedule and live life at her own pace.

But she hadn't counted on setting down new roots so quickly. She was going to miss her friends here when the time to leave came.

"So," Violet said after a moment.

Flora looked over at her friend and raised her eyebrows. "So?"

"You and Grady."

She waited, but nothing followed that statement but silence and a sharp look. "Me and Grady what?"

"Don't give me that. Are you two dating? I've been wondering for a while, but I just can't figure it out."

Flora blinked, then laughed. "No, we aren't dating. We're just friends. He was the first person I really connected with here, other than you. He's one of the best people I know, but I don't think he likes me like *that*, and I don't have time to date. Especially not when I'm going to be moving away in less than two years."

Violet's eyes narrowed. "Okay, first, I'm pretty sure he *is* interested in you. Whenever we're all together, he can't take his eyes off of you. He goes out of his way to help you, and he never lets you pay him for anything, does he? He's a handyman — I know he works at the hardware store, but he also does odd jobs around town, and I can guarantee you he would charge anyone else a *lot* for all that work he did with you on your shed. He's definitely interested in you, Flora. I know you aren't *that* blind."

Flora frowned. "He's never asked me out or said anything about it. And you're making it sound like he's only been helping me because he wants to date me, which isn't fair to either of us. He wouldn't do all of that expecting something in return — I know him better than that."

"I didn't say he was. I don't think he expects anything, he just likes spending time with you. Really, Flora, if you're this oblivious I'm not surprised he hasn't made a move. He probably thinks you aren't interested in him, and he's too nice to make you uncomfortable."

"But you aren't?" she grumbled.

Violet grinned. "Nope. Someone needed to say it, and that someone was me. Besides, you're both friends of mine, and this intervention is going to help you both because I don't think his interest is one-sided."

"Look, I like Grady, and if circumstances were normal, sure — I'd go out with him if he asked. He's cute, and kind, and I trust him. I'm not going to lie, I like watching him lift stuff when he's wearing one of those sleeveless shirts. But not only did I just get out of a bad relationship, I'm *leaving* in a year and a half. It wouldn't be fair to either of us to start something serious."

"Girl, you are being ridiculous. You don't have to marry the guy. Aren't you planning on doing this house flipping thing for the foreseeable future? Are you really planning on not dating anyone, ever, just because you're going to move every few years?" Violet sighed. "I like you, Flora. You're a good person, and one of the bravest women I know. But you're a little silly sometimes. I'm *telling* you Grady likes you, and I already know you feel the same about him. Get your head out of the sand and make a move before you regret not doing so. He knows you're not going to be here forever. But that doesn't mean you can't have fun while you *are* here. Besides, you don't know what's going to happen. Maybe the housing market will crash and you'll have to stay for a couple years longer, or maybe you'll find the perfect house somewhere nearby to flip when you're done with this one. You can't put your life on hold forever."

"You've been holding this in for a long time, haven't you?" Flora asked. At her friend's glare, she raised her hands. "All right, all right. I'll think about what you said. That's all I'll promise."

"Good."

Violet sniffed and then raised her glass of lemonade to her lips. Flora leaned back in her chair and gazed out at the rolling hills across the dirt road. Maybe she was being a bit of an idiot, but did she really want to risk having her heart broken again? Even if she did start dating Grady, there would be an end-date built into their relationship. Leaving her friends would be hard enough, but she didn't know if she could stomach the thought of leaving someone she had fallen in love with.

CHAPTER TWO

Violet's conversation was still on Flora's mind when Grady's truck pulled into the driveway the next morning. She heard it approaching before it reached her house, and was out on the porch in time to see it bounce over the pot hole at the end of her driveway. She winced. Violet wasn't the only one who was bad at avoiding the thing, but Grady didn't seem to care.

She was a little annoyed at Violet, not for her 'intervention,' but for the timing of it. She and Grady were going to spend all day working on her driveway, and she just knew she was going to be distracted by what her friend had said.

She tried to push it out of her mind as she walked down the porch steps to meet him as he got out of his truck.

"Hey," he said. "You ready to go?"

"Yep. I'm glad we're finally doing this. I'll finally be able to use my driveway without my poor truck rattling all over the place." She paused. "You'll have to move your truck to the side, I don't think I can pull mine out around it."

"I thought we'd use mine," he told her.

"Won't putting a bunch of rocks in the bed scuff it up?" she asked.

He raised a single eyebrow and made a show of looking between their two trucks. Hers, shiny and white and only a few years old. His, red and rusty and probably almost as old as she was, and with as many dents as it had years.

"I think my truck can survive a few more scratches."

"Fair enough. Let me go grab my purse. Do you want a water bottle?"

At his nod, she ducked back into her house to grab the water bottles from the fridge and to snag her purse from the counter. She bent down to run her hand along Amaretto's spine, the cat's fluffy tail trailing across her arm before she straightened up.

"We'll be back in about an hour. See you in a little bit, princess."

She had to block the door with her legs as she slipped out, and when she glanced back after walking down the porch steps, she saw Amaretto in the window, gazing out at her with narrowed eyes. She knew that if she could see the cat's tail from this angle, the tip of it would be twitching back and forth.

No, Amaretto was not happy being stuck inside the house all the time. Maybe she needed more toys, or better yet, a way she could safely go outside. Flora had tried putting a harness on her before and the cat hadn't been a fan, but she decided to try again.

Wouldn't she be a sight, walking up and down her rural dirt road with her fluffy white cat on a leash?

Grady started his truck again as she got into the passenger seat. After putting the water bottles in the cup holder and her purse on the floor by her seat, she put her seatbelt on and gazed out the window at her house as the truck pulled away from it.

It already looked much better than it had when she bought it. A new roof, a fresh coat of paint on the siding, the red and white flowers in the beds that wrapped around the house… the new gravel would really bring it all together. She still had a lot of work to do on the interior, but seeing the progress always filled her with a sense of pride.

"So, you know the person we're buying the gravel from?" Flora asked as they drove down the road towards town.

"He's an old buddy of my brother's. Decent guy. Bought the gravel lot about fifteen years ago. He's got the best prices in the area, and might give us a discount since he knows me."

"Oh, good." She paused. "Um, not to be rude… but isn't your brother in prison? I'm not sure how good of a recommendation that is."

He snorted. "Yeah. I guess that might not be reassuring. But Connor was a work friend, someone Wade met while he was trying to start up a business a while back. He was never involved with the drugs."

"Is that what your brother's in prison for?"

"He was arrested for possession with the intent to sell." Grady sighed. "He got pulled over and the police found a stash in the back of his car."

"Huh. I thought you said it was a DUI, back when we first met."

"That was part of it," he said, looking embarrassed. "That's the reason the police had for pulling him over in the first place, and he tested a little over the legal limit, but it's not what got him most of his sentence. It's just easier to explain it as a DUI, and I didn't know you back then. I didn't mean to mislead you, but I don't usually go around talking about all of this to strangers. You're not a stranger anymore, though."

"No, I get it. You don't have to explain every single facet of your brother's history to everyone you meet. It doesn't really matter, anyway, since you said Connor wasn't involved in any of it."

"Right," he said. "He'll give you a good price, and that's all that really matters for this. You'll get your nice new driveway in no time at all."

She nodded, relaxing back into the seat. She knew Grady came from a very different world than she did, but most of the time, it was easy to forget about.

Sometimes, however, the differences between an upper-class city girl and a small-town guy who had grown up in a trailer park were hard to ignore. She trusted him, though, and it wasn't like she was going to the gravel lot alone. He would be by her side the entire time.

The gravel lot was a few miles north of town. Flora had seen the piles of gravel and dirt as she drove past, but this was the first time she had ever actually gone there. Grady pulled into the driveway, past the open gates, and parked in front of the small office building. There were a couple of backhoes and front loaders parked near the building, and she saw someone using one of them to load some road gravel into a trailer.

"Let's head into the office, see who's in," Grady said as he turned off his truck.

Flora got out of the cab with her purse and the two of them walked up to the building. An open sign was on the outside of the door, and she could hear voices coming from inside. She pushed it open and stepped into an argument.

"…getting another survey! Everything past the trees at the west edge of your property is *mine.*"

"Look, Lacie, I showed you the property lines from the surveyor I hired back when I bought this place. I own another hundred feet out, and this parcel is zoned industrial, so some noise is to be expected. I understand it's upsetting to see the trees cut down, but I need more storage space. There's already been enough of a delay while you hired your surveyor. It's not my fault she quit out of the blue. I can't delay any longer. I'm going to start removing trees next week. My offer for you to take some of the lumber still—"

"I don't want the trees you cut down! Those are *my trees.*"

Flora exchanged a look with Grady. They edged into the small building and let the door fall shut behind them. The woman who was facing off against the burly man behind the counter turned to look at them before turning back around to continue her argument. Her face was flushed, and she kept clenching and relaxing her fists.

"If you cut down a single one, you will see me in court. Don't push me, Connor. I know my rights, and my family has owned this land for longer than either of us have been alive. I think I know my own property line a bit better than you do."

With that, she spun on her heel and walked past them, yanking the door open and striding out into the sunlight. There was a moment of silence before the man behind the counter cleared his throat.

"Sorry about that. Good to see you, Grady. How can I help you?"

Flora knew he was probably directing his words to Grady because he was the one he knew, but she felt a sting of annoyance at being dismissed right away. She knew she didn't exactly look like someone who was here to buy a truckload of gravel, but the man had hardly even glanced at her.

"I'm here to buy marble chips for my driveway," she said, taking half a step forward.

"I see," he said, glancing toward her. "Will you need it delivered? How much are you looking for?"

"We're just loading it into my pickup," Grady said. "One load should be enough, but we can come back if we need more."

"All right. Let me page Jamie, he's fulfilling an order for someone else but he should be done soon, and he's already got the backhoe warmed up."

She waited as he called his employee, then rang up her order. She was in the process of paying when the door to the small building opened and a younger man, who looked to be around twenty, came in.

"We got another order, Connor?" he asked.

"Yep. Grady and his lady friend need some crushed marble. Take them to the pile on the east side of the lot and fill 'em up." He handed Flora's card back over. "They've paid already. I'll see you around, Grady. Good luck with your project."

Flora frowned a little at being relegated to "Grady's lady friend," but didn't say anything as she put her card back into the wallet, grabbed her purse, and followed him and Jamie outside.

"I'll hop into the backhoe. Just follow me," Jamie said.

She slipped into the truck's passenger seat and Grady started the engine. They followed Jamie in the backhoe through the gravel yard, until the backhoe braked. It started beeping and slowly backing up, so Grady put the truck into reverse to give it room to maneuver. Jamie backed the backhoe up until he could turn around, and headed off into the opposite direction of the one they had been going in. Flora glanced over as they drove past and saw that the path was blocked by a front loader someone had left parked between two big piles of gravel.

Jamie stopped the backhoe by a large, white mound of marble chips near the edge of the property. There were some weeds growing on one side of it, and the paths between the gravel hills were a little overgrown.

He got out of the backhoe to direct them as Grady backed up toward the gravel and to check the bed of the truck.

"Sorry about the detour," he said through Flora's open window. "I think Kevin left that front loader there when he went on his break, and I didn't want to keep you while I moved it. This stuff is a little older, but it'll do you fine. Just sit tight and don't get out of your truck until you see me wave at you."

He climbed back into the backhoe and Flora turned in her seat to watch as he scooped up a load of gravel and carefully emptied it into the truck bed. She could feel the truck shifting with the added weight. When he was done, he honked on the horn and waved cheerfully before driving the backhoe away.

"That was easy," she said as she got out of the truck. Grady reached into the back of the cab to grab the tarp and ratchet straps.

"Costs a lot less to have them load it up here and unload yourself," he said. "We're in for some hard work when we get back to the house, though."

She helped him throw the tarp over the gravel and tie it down so none of the stones flew out while they were driving. As she rounded the back of the truck, she glanced over at the hill of gravel behind her, and her steps faltered.

"Grady?"

"Hmm?"

"What is that?"

He pulled the last strap tight, then came over to look at the hill of gravel. A few stones tumbled down, having been disturbed by the backhoe, but that wasn't what her eyes were glued to.

She couldn't stop staring at something that was buried deep in the hill of gravel, something the backhoe had exposed when it scooped the chipped marble out.

A human arm was sticking out of the pile of stones.

CHAPTER THREE

Grady rushed forward, climbing the gravel hill until he could brush bits of stone away from the body. Flora followed him more slowly, a sick feeling making her stomach clench. Grady's digging revealed the person's shoulder and then torso. Flora saw long hair, dusty from the stone. It was evident that the woman had been dead for a while.

"Stop," she whispered. "You should stop. We have to call the police."

He stopped digging through the stones, stepping back to look down at the body in horror.

Flora remembered he didn't have a cell phone, so she hurried back to the truck to take hers out of the cab.

Her hands were shaking as she dialed the emergency number.

When the dispatcher answered, she had to step around the back of the truck to get the name of the gravel lot and the address from Grady. He must have seen how upset she was, because he put his hand on her shoulder and squeezed.

They waited there next to the body for the police to arrive. No one else disturbed them. She could hear the sound of heavy equipment running elsewhere in the lot, but the two of them were alone in their little corner of it. The sound of sirens announced the arrival of the authorities, and she heard shouting voices in the distance, followed by the crunch of tires on gravel as a vehicle navigated the path toward them. She realized the dispatcher was talking in her ear, asking her to describe where exactly in the lot they were, and she handed the phone over to Grady so he could direct them. She didn't feel like she was thinking straight. She turned to stare at the half-unburied body, feeling cold despite the warmth of the day.

For once, Officer Hendricks wasn't the one who responded to the call. She was a little relieved, since she knew he would have had a *look* on his face when he realized she had once again found herself in the middle of what seemed likely to be a homicide investigation, but at least she knew him. She would rather see him than the strangers she saw step out of the police cruiser when it pulled up in front of Grady's truck.

What followed was a blur. One of the officers had her and Grady step to the side before joining his partner in examining the body in the gravel. Jamie and Connor had followed the police vehicle in another pickup truck and both stood watching from a distance.

Jamie looked horrified. Connor's expression was more unreadable, but his face was grim and his arms were crossed over his chest.

Slowly, the officers continued to excavate the woman's body. Flora couldn't watch, and focused on watching sparrows chase each other around a tree instead, until Grady jolted beside her.

"What is it?" she murmured to him.

"I know her," he whispered. "Her name is Audrey. She used to work at the hardware shop. She quit about three years ago because she got a better paying job."

"Did she work *here*?" Flora asked.

He shook his head. "I don't think so, but I don't remember exactly what she said she was going to do. Mr. Brant might know."

Flora winced at the thought of trying to shout questions to the nearly deaf old man and turned her attention back to the sparrows while Grady continued to watch as the police brushed the stone away from the woman's body.

Eventually, one of the officers came to talk with them. Flora and Grady told their story, about how they had come here to get gravel for Flora's driveway, how Jamie had filled the truck for them, and how they had noticed the arm sticking out of the gravel.

It was nearly an hour before they were cleared to leave, which was when they got bad news – they couldn't take the gravel with them. Since it was part of the same pile of gravel the body had been found in, there might be evidence buried in it somewhere. The police helped her and Grady shovel it all out of the bed of the truck, and warned them it might be as long as a couple of weeks before the gravel lot would be open for business again.

Flora couldn't even be disappointed. She felt numb as they got into the truck and Grady navigated to the lot's exit. A police cruiser was sitting at the entrance to the lot, turning other customers away. The woman behind the wheel waved at them as they pulled onto the main road.

And then, they were alone and on their way home.

"I hate this," Flora murmured. "That poor woman. I wonder how long she was buried there?"

"It has to have been recent," Grady said. "She wasn't a skeleton."

"The gravel might have kept away insects and pests, though," Flora mused. "It didn't look like anyone had used that part of the lot for a long time. Maybe it was an accident – maybe she was climbing around on the gravel hills for some reason, fell, and got covered by it."

"She wouldn't have been buried so deep if that's what happened," Grady said.

Flora sighed. "I know. I just hate the thought that someone killed her and hid her there on purpose."

"I don't think you can find another explanation that makes sense. It takes heavy machinery to move that much gravel. Either that, or a few hours and a lot of sweat with a shovel. There's no way she ended up there accidentally."

"Do you think Jamie knew she was there?" Flora asked quietly.

"If he did, why would he have exposed her?"

"Maybe he was *trying* to expose her," she suggested. "I mean, out of all of the piles of gravel in the lot, he chose that one. He wasn't even supposed to take us there – it sounded like Connor asked him to take us to a different pile of marble chips, but that front loader was in the way, remember?"

"I do," Grady said. He put on his blinker to turn into town. "But I doubt Jamie knew anything about her. It makes me think that Connor might have known, though."

"I thought he was a friend of yours," Flora said, frowning. "Do you really think he might be behind this?"

"I have known him for years, and I trust him not to rip me off if I need to buy some stone from his lot, but he isn't a close friend, not in the way you are with Violet. I don't know him well enough to say there's no way he hid a body on his property." He frowned too. "Don't go back there without me, all right?"

"I won't," she promised.

"I wish I could remember where Audrey said her new job was," Grady said with a sigh. "I thought it had something to do with construction or yardwork, so maybe she did work there. I suppose it doesn't matter; knowing where she worked won't tell us what happened to her, and the cops will figure all of that out anyway."

"Do you remember her last name? I could look her up online," Flora suggested.

"Ayers," he said. "Her name was Audrey Ayers."

She opened her social media app on her phone and typed in the name. When the results came up, she turned the screen toward Grady so he could indicate which profile was hers. She clicked on the woman's picture and scrolled through her page. Either she hadn't posted a lot or most of her settings were turned to private, but the *About* section listed her employment status.

"Wow, she worked at the hardware store for five years. You must've known her pretty well." She scrolled down a little more. "Here it is. She was working for Bronson Surveying." Flora frowned, exchanging a look with Grady who seemed to have realized the same thing she had.

"That's quite the coincidence," he muttered.

"I think it might be more than a coincidence. Didn't Connor say the surveyor that lady hired disappeared before she finished the job? What if Audrey was the surveyor? And she didn't drop the ball on the job — she was killed?"

CHAPTER FOUR

Grady stayed with her at her house for a couple of hours when they got back. He held the ladder while she painted the patched plaster in the ceiling of the second-floor bedroom where the roof had leaked. Fixing that had been a job and a half, and Flora had spent a few days after it was done with an aching back, shoulders, and neck from the awkward position she had to be in to work on the ceiling, but the room looked much better now that it was done.

Usually, they chatted and laughed while they worked, but today was somber. Not only had someone died, but it was someone Grady knew, someone he had worked with for years. Flora wasn't sure what to say.

She also wasn't sure what to say about Connor's possible involvement in the murder. He might not be a close friend of Grady's, but he had known him for a long time.

Flora held out a quiet hope that the woman's death might have been an accident somehow. She knew it was improbable, but she spent her time painting trying to figure out how it could have happened. Maybe she had been doing her survey work at the gravel yard and had somehow gotten injured on the pile of marble chips, and one of the employees had failed to notice her laying on the hill of gravel before loading more rocks onto it.

Piecing together theories in her mind made the time go by, but it didn't help. All she and Grady could do was hope that the police investigation would be a swift one.

Since she wasn't going to be fixing her driveway for the foreseeable future, Flora decided to tackle painting the upstairs bedrooms. Her aunt was going to come over for Thanksgiving in just a couple of months, and Flora wanted to have at least one of the rooms ready for her. That meant removing the old wallpaper, painting the walls and the trim, making sure the windows weren't too drafty, and sanding and re-staining the hardwood floors. She also needed to buy furniture and decor for what would become the guest room. That would be her reward for finishing everything else.

After Grady left with a promise to keep her updated if he heard anything about the case from Connor or any of his other friends, she got her can of white paint and started on the trim in the upstairs bedroom. She kept the door to the bedroom closed so Amaretto couldn't join her. She felt bad for keeping the cat in the hallway, but Amaretto's tail was like a paintbrush, and she didn't need her furry companion getting white paint all over everything.

While Amaretto meowed and swiped her paws under the door frame, Flora started sanding and then repainting the trim in the room. That kept her busy until the evening, when she took a well-deserved break and tried to relax. It felt strange to be sitting in the living room, eating some leftover casserole from Beth in front of her TV after what had happened that morning, but what were the alternatives? She couldn't *do* anything. She didn't know any of the people involved, and it wasn't like she could go back to the gravel yard with a magnifying glass and a notebook and try to solve the crime on her own. All she could do was wait and focus on her own life in the meantime.

While she ate her breakfast the next morning, she went through some paint swatches from the hardware store. After some deliberation, she settled on a light, gray-blue color for the guest room upstairs. Blue, she knew, was supposed to be a calming color, and the shade was mild enough most people should either like it or not feel strongly about it. It would also be easy for someone to paint over if they wanted to change it when she sold the house.

Grady hadn't called her with news, and she couldn't find anything about Audrey Ayers' death online, other than for one post in the local group asking what had happened and why there were police at the gravel lot the day before, so, with nothing else to do, she grabbed her purse and got into her truck, heading for town to buy the paint. She was excited to be getting another room done. When she finally started working on the floors, she knew her progress would slow down, because she hadn't yet tackled any of the hardwood floors in the house and would have to learn how to do it as she went. She could hardly wait to see what they would look like after they were sanded and re-stained, with a nice shine to them.

She was expecting to see Grady at the hardware store. She had his work schedule memorized by now, and he told her whenever it changed, but the only one working when she got there that day was old Mr. Brant. She shouted a hello to the mostly deaf older man before going to look for the paint. Even though she hadn't seen Grady's truck parked outside, she kept her eyes peeled for him, but he wasn't anywhere in the store.

She was a little worried, though she told herself she was being ridiculous. Nothing could possibly have happened to him between when she saw him yesterday and this morning. Or, something *could* have, but she would have heard about a bad car accident or a fire at the trailer park. He hadn't seemed sick yesterday, and she had never known him to take a day off without warning, so where *was* he?

She found the cans of semigloss paint she wanted and waited while Mr. Brant mixed them so they would match her paint swatch, then did the only thing she could do; paid and left the store. She carried her two cans of paint out to her truck and debated on going to the coffee shop for some coffee. She'd already had some coffee for breakfast, so she didn't need the caffeine, and when she drove past the coffee shop, it was busy. She was eager to get home and start the wallpaper removal process, because the sooner she finished with that, the sooner she would be able to paint, so she passed it by reluctantly and headed for home.

She was just about to turn onto her road when her cell phone rang. She glanced down at where it sat in one of the cupholders and reached for it automatically when she saw Grady's name. He didn't have a cell phone, so the only way he could communicate with her was through his home phone. Even so, he rarely called – she went to the hardware store often enough that any arrangements for projects they were working on could be made in person. She hit the button to answer the call, connecting it to her truck's Bluetooth, and said, "Hello?"

"Hey, Flora," he said. "Could you do me a favor?"

"Of course," she said. "What happened? Are you all right? I stopped at the hardware store, but you weren't there."

"I was about to leave for work this morning when someone knocked on my door. He says he's Audrey's boyfriend, and Connor told him you and I were the ones who found the body. He has some theories, and I thought you should hear them too. Are you interested in talking to him?"

"Definitely," she said, not bothering to hide her curiosity. "Are you still at home? Of course you are, you're calling from your home phone. Do you want me to come over?"

She had never seen Grady's trailer and was more than a little curious about it.

"Would you mind if we come over to your place?"

Of course. She sighed. "No, that's fine. I tidied it just a couple of days ago, though I can't say I have much in the way of snacks or drinks other than lemonade right now. I'm just getting home myself. When do you think you'll be here?"

"In about twenty minutes, unless that's too soon."

"It's fine. That will give me time to bring everything in and get ready for a guest. See you soon."

She ended the call, intrigued to learn what this was all about. She supposed she would find out soon enough. Besides, she was also more than a little glad to put off the task of removing all of the wallpaper in the guest bedroom.

She hated removing wallpaper.

CHAPTER FIVE

She got everything ready in the upstairs bedroom so she could start work as soon as Grady and her mysterious visitor left and managed to make a fresh pitcher of lemonade before they arrived. They didn't drive together – Grady's truck was the first to rattle over her pothole, then an old hatchback followed suit. She winced as she heard the vehicle bottom out over the gravel. It wasn't her fault. She had tried to fix the driveway, she was just utterly cursed when it came to plans going off without a hitch.

She scooped Amaretto up into her arms before she opened the door for her guests. The cat struggled in her grip and Flora winced as her back claws dug into the skin over her ribcage. It was time to do that very disliked chore again. She knew she would have more than a few new scratches on her skin by the time she finished trimming the cat's nails, but if Amaretto was going to be this bad about being kept from the outdoors, it was necessary.

"Hey," she said to Grady and the stranger who followed him onto her porch. "Come on in."

She stepped back to let them through the door. As she did so, she observed the man Grady had brought with him. He was tall, taller than Grady even, with a thick build and short, black hair. He looked tough, but his eyes were red rimmed and he walked with such a defeated slouch that she immediately felt bad for him.

"Thanks for letting us come over," Grady said. "This is Flint. Flint, this is Flora, the woman who was with me yesterday."

"Sorry to disturb you like this," Flint said.

"It's no problem at all," Flora said. She shut the door and set her cat down. Amaretto crouched close to the floor, looked up at the stranger with wide yellow eyes, and then darted off somewhere else into the house. "I am curious as to why you're here. Do you know Grady?"

"No," the man said. "I guess he didn't tell you much over the phone."

"Come on," she said, tamping down her curiosity temporarily. "Let's sit in the living room. I'll pour everyone some lemonade while you tell me what's going on."

She got three glasses and met the men in the living room. Flint had taken the armchair, so she and Grady both sat on the couch. She passed the lemonade around, then looked expectantly at Flint, who cleared his throat.

"Well, yesterday evening I got a call from my girl-friend's – Audrey's – mother telling me her body had been found at the gravel lot. No one seemed to know anything, and I spent all night trying to figure out what was going on. This morning, I had enough of not knowing anything, so I drove down to the gravel lot myself. I… I was pretty upset. It was early and the place was still closed, but Connor was there. We went to high school together. We weren't friends, but… we know each other well enough he was willing to talk to me, I guess. He didn't say much, though. Just that Grady Barnes and some woman he didn't know had found a body in one of his gravel piles. Then he told me to get off the property and not come back, and that no one was supposed to be there. It took some doing to track down Grady. I caught him at his trailer right before he left for work and asked him to tell me everything that happened yesterday. He was a lot more helpful than Connor, that's for sure."

"You deserve to know what happened," Grady said. "That's not why we came over here, though."

"Grady thought you might be interested in something I said to him," Flint said hesitantly. "He said… well, that you're smart, and you've figured out some things the cops missed before."

Flora raised an eyebrow and glanced over at Grady, who looked embarrassed. "Sort of. It was all mostly luck. I think I just have a knack for making connections."

"Well, I want to find out what happened to Audrey. The cops are already working on her case, but more people trying to put it all together can't hurt." He took a deep breath. "I know Audrey was surveying the lot that the gravel business is on. There was some sort of property dispute between the owner of the gravel lot and one of his neighbors. Audrey had worked as a surveyor for the past couple of years, and she doesn't talk about her assignments very much. Most of them are boring. She talked about this one because it was so interesting. You see, she was hired by the person whose property borders the gravel lot, but her first day on the job, she told me the gravel lot's owner approached her. He offered to pay her quite a lot of money to make sure her report reflected no changes to the property line in question."

Flora's eyebrows climbed up her forehead. "Connor was trying to bribe her?"

Grady had a grim expression on his face. "That's what it sounds like." They exchanged a look. He might not be a close friend of Connor's, but she knew he didn't want the man to be Audrey's killer, any more than Flora would want to face the thought that one of her old acquaintances was a murderer.

"She refused," Flint said. "And then, a week later, she stopped replying to my calls or texts. That was five days ago."

"Have you told the police about this?" Flora asked. It wasn't physical evidence that Connor had killed her, but it certainly seemed like the sort of circumstantial evidence that could get the police a warrant to search his things, if they didn't have one already.

"Not yet," Flint said. "I told Grady I would go to the police station after stopping by here. I just... Audrey was a good person. She never would have accepted a bribe, and she wouldn't have hesitated to submit the correct survey findings even if she knew what she found would make Connor mad. I know police investigations don't move as quickly in real life as they do on TV. It could be months before the man faces any sort of justice. Grady seems to think you are some sort of miracle worker. So please, if you can do anything, do it. Get Audrey the justice she deserves."

Flora leaned back against the couch cushions. That was... a lot. "I'm sorry, but I really don't know what I could do," she said. "I can ask around, see if any of my friends have heard anything, but despite what Grady said, I'm not some sort of secret, superpowered private investigator. I'm just... an ex-accountant who wanted to learn how to flip houses."

"The more people who are looking out for her, the better," Flint said firmly. "I already failed her once. It's too late to save her, but I'll do whatever it takes to figure out what happened."

"What do you mean by that?" Flora asked. "That you already failed her once."

Flint looked away, his lips curling downwards. "I didn't hear from her for four days before she was found," he muttered. "Complete radio silence, and I didn't tell anyone. Not her family, not her friends, not even the police. She was dead for four days and no one even knew she was missing because I didn't say a thing."

CHAPTER SIX

Flint excused himself after that, muttering something about going to the police station to tell them what he had told her. Grady stayed behind, waiting until Flint left before he turned to Flora.

"Sorry about that," he said. "I thought you would be interested in hearing what he has to say, but I didn't think he was going to put all of that on you."

"It's okay," she said. "He's grieving. I can understand that." She frowned. "I do think it's a little odd that she was missing for so long and he didn't say anything to anyone. They were dating. If any one of my friends went silent for more than a day or two, I would start looking for them."

Grady shrugged. "Maybe they had a fight beforehand," he suggested. "I don't know. He seemed genuinely upset, though."

She sighed. "Yeah." She shot a glance towards the stairs. The wallpaper awaited her. Removing it was a slow process, which involved soaking the walls and slowly scraping the paper off. It was time-consuming and annoying to do, but at least it would be a distraction. She felt guilty now, though she knew what happened to Audrey was in no way her fault. She didn't feel guilty for the woman's *death*, but rather for not doing more to try to figure out what happened to her.

It wasn't her job, she knew that, but someone had asked her for help. How could she ignore that?

She glanced at Grady. "Are you going to work now?"

He shook his head. "Mr. Brant told me to take the day off after I called to let him know I would be late."

She grinned. "Want to help me with the wallpaper upstairs? We can talk while we work. I don't know if we can be as helpful as Flint seems to hope we will be, but a little bit of brainstorming can't hurt. If

Connor *did* kill her, there has to be some way to prove it."

"Sure," he said. He gave her a small smile. "I never thought I would be trying to solve a murder while removing wallpaper. Life sure has gotten interesting since you moved here, Flora."

She heaved an overly dramatic sigh. "Don't remind me. Officer Hendricks already thinks I'm cursed. I don't need the universe to keep trying to convince me that it's true."

Grady's help made the wallpaper removal go faster, both because she had another set of hands helping her, and because the company made time fly by. They talked a little about Connor and Grady's experiences with him over the years. He had never known the man to have a violent temper, and nothing he said made Connor stand out as a potential murderer, but Flora knew it wasn't as simple as that. People could change, or they could hide who they were. Murderers didn't always look or even act the part. Sometimes, maybe even usually, they seemed just like everyone else until their crimes came to light.

They ordered a pizza for dinner and ate it at Flora's kitchen table while Amaretto watched from her own chair, her tail flicking back and forth. The cat was annoyed at being shut away from them all day, and Flora resolved to pick up some new toys and a harness for her at the feed store tomorrow. She needed to get some more cat food anyway, and she didn't want Amaretto to be bored.

The thought reminded her of a text message she had gotten from Violet earlier. "Oh," she said between bites of pizza. "Violet and I are meeting for lunch at the sandwich shop tomorrow. Do you want to join us?"

"I'll be working," he said. "I can't afford to take more time off after today."

"I'll bring you a sandwich, then," she promised before taking another bite of her crust. Grady looked a little surprised, but oddly pleased. She remembered Violet's conversation with her just a few days ago. It felt like longer, with everything that had happened since.

What were Grady's feelings toward her? She didn't think she could ask him straight to his face, not when she wasn't even sure what *her* feelings toward him were. When she hugged him goodbye that evening, she focused on how it felt. His arms around her felt good. Safe. She liked hugging him, but she had spent so long thinking that she wouldn't be dating anyone anytime soon that she wasn't sure if she liked hugging him because he was her friend, or if there was something more.

She waved as he pulled out of the driveway and was still deep in thought as she shut and locked her front door.

Maybe Violet had a point. She couldn't just never date again, and if she was serious about flipping houses, she was going to be moving around a lot for the foreseeable future. She didn't have to move to a new town every time, and her plan had been to relocate somewhere closer to Chicago once she got some experience under her belt with a cheaper house. But... maybe it wouldn't be the end of the world to date someone in the meantime. She had plans for the future, but none of them were set in stone. If she did start dating Grady and it got serious, she could stay around here for the next couple of years, couldn't she? Even if she moved to a bigger town in Kentucky, she could always come back and see him regularly. She can do an hour's drive every weekend easily to keep up with her friends here.

Sighing, she went into the kitchen to feed Amaretto. In some ways, her life seemed simple. She had to fix up the house, and that was it. In other ways, it just kept getting more and more complicated.

She got a little more work done on the wallpaper in the guest room the next morning before she headed into town. She stopped at the feed store first and said hi to Sydney after she got the supplies for her cat. She spent a few minutes chatting with him, catching him up on what had happened at the gravel lot. She hadn't seen her friends as much as usual over the past couple of weeks. Their work schedules kept conflicting with each other, and she and Grady had been busy working on the shed. She hoped that would change soon. She missed getting together with all of them at once.

After saying goodbye to Sydney, she drove to the small sandwich shop that was just down the road from Violet Delights. Violet had walked over there for her lunch break, and was waiting outside the building. She waved cheerfully as Flora got out of her truck, and the two of them walked into the sandwich shop together. Flora looked over the menu before ordering the French dip, and Violet got a fried bologna sandwich with shredded lettuce, honey mustard, muenster cheese, and house-made potato chips on it. Flora was morbidly curious to see what the end result looked like. They took their order numbers and went to find a secluded table in the back of the restaurant.

"I'm glad we could meet today," Violet said. "I was talking to Sydney last night. It sounds like he works the morning shift on Friday. I know Grady is always out by seven when he works, and I'll be done by then too. Do you want to get together Friday night? Not to volunteer your house or anything, but we could have a bonfire, maybe do a cookout?"

Flora grinned, sipping her soda. "I was just thinking about how we all needed to get together again soon," she said. "That sounds great. I'll let Grady know."

Violet grinned at her. "Speaking of Grady, have you thought about what I said?"

"I've been kind of busy, what with finding a body and all," Flora murmured, keeping her voice low. She rolled her eyes reluctantly. "But yes. I... I do like him. I think I want to figure out if he feels the same way. I'm mostly just worried it will change things."

"Of course it'll change things, but for the better," Violet said. "The two of you will be great together. Anyone who has seen you together can tell."

"Please tell me you haven't been talking about this with Sydney." Flora groaned.

"Flora, don't be silly." Her friend grinned even wider. "I talk about everything with Sydney. You and Grady are always off in your own little world. It only makes sense that Sydney and I would turn to each other for comfort when we've been so cruelly abandoned by you two."

It was Flora's turn to give Violet a sharp grin. "So you're turning to each other for *comfort*, huh? Did I miss something? Are the two of *you* dating?"

To her surprise, her friend, who was usually so unflappable, blushed. "We might have gone out on one or two dates," she admitted. "But we aren't exclusive and we haven't really told anyone."

"Oh." Flora blinked. "I was just kidding, but I'm happy for you. My lips are sealed."

"Thanks. You can tell Grady, of course, but we don't want to make a big thing of it until we know where it's going."

"No wonder you've been pushing me about Grady," Flora said. "It makes more sense now."

"I do think the two of you would be happy together," Violet said. "But I don't mean to push you into anything."

"No, it's all right," Flora said. "I didn't mean it in a bad way. I think I did need a little bit of a push."

"Well, enough about all this," Violet said suddenly. "Have you heard anything else about the murder?" She whispered the last word. Flora opened her mouth to answer but paused when she saw the waitress approaching with their food. She accepted her French dip gratefully and eyed the sandwich Violet had ordered. To her surprise, it looked pretty good. She hadn't had fried bologna since she was a kid, and realized she might have misjudged what a decent sandwich restaurant could do with the ingredient.

She took a bite of her French dip and waited until she was done chewing to tell Violet about Flint's visit the day before. Her friend listened with interest, munching away on her sandwich.

"It sounds like it's definitely someone who works at the gravel lot," Violet said at last. "I mean, it would need to be, wouldn't it? They would have to have access to heavy equipment to bury her there."

"Or a shovel and a lot of time," Flora said, thinking of Grady saying almost those exact same words a couple of days ago.

"It's a shame that Grady's friend is the most likely suspect," Violet mused. "It's always hard to admit that someone you know might not be the person they thought you were."

Violet had personal experience with that. Flora patted her hand sympathetically. "I know. I keep holding out hope that it's someone else. Who knows, maybe one of his employees did it."

"It is a little suspicious that one employee who helped you just happened to lead you directly to the pile of gravel that had a dead body in it."

"Grady and I talked about that," Flora said. "It *is* a little suspicious, but neither of us can think of a reason he would lead us there on purpose if he had something to do with her death." She sighed. "No, it almost has to be Connor. He has it all – the motive, the means... We just have to wait for the police to get the evidence they need to put him behind bars."

It seemed like an open and shut case to her. She just hoped that it was as simple as it seemed, and Audrey would get her justice as soon as possible.

CHAPTER SEVEN

However, the days continued to pass by with no news about Audrey's case. In fact, there was very little about it posted online at all. Flora wondered if the police were keeping it under wraps on purpose, or if Warbler's gossip mill had just somehow missed news of the woman's death. Flora finished removing the wallpaper and sanding the walls down Wednesday afternoon, and spent Wednesday evening painting a coat of white primer over the walls. Between the repaired ceiling and the fresh, white walls and trim, the room looked much better, if somewhat barren.

She woke up bright and early on Thursday, ridiculously excited to finally start painting *color* on the walls. She fed Amaretto, tossed one of the cat's new toys around a little bit, and spent a few minutes feeding her treats while settling the first loop of the harness over Amaretto's head. Once Amaretto seemed sufficiently entertained, she went upstairs and started painting.

She was halfway through the first coat of paint when her phone, which had been blasting music on a portable Bluetooth speaker, started ringing with an incoming call instead. She put the paint roller down in the tray and wiped her hands off on a spare rag before picking up the phone. It was a local number, but not one she had saved to her contact list. Curious, she answered it.

"Hello?"

"I'm calling for a Flora Abner?" a male voice said over the line. The voice sounded familiar, but she couldn't place it.

"Speaking," she said. "May I ask who's calling?"

"This is Connor from the gravel lot. I'm calling to let you know we have officially reopened. I saw that your order was still unfulfilled. You are welcome to come pick up your gravel at any time."

"Oh." She hadn't forgotten about the gravel, but she hadn't been expecting the lot to reopen so soon, or to get a call when they did. "Thank you for letting me know. I'll try to come get it soon."

"Yep. Have a good day."

Connor ended the call. She blinked at her phone. Part of her wondered if he even recognized her name. He had completely dismissed her when she was there with Grady, and she got the feeling he was the sort of man who didn't tend to think much of woman's abilities to do things on their own.

She hit the button to start playing the music again and picked up her paint roller. As she resumed painting the walls, she wondered what she should do. She still wanted to fix up her driveway, of course. She *needed* to. The potholes were only going to get worse, and a poorly maintained driveway wouldn't do her any favors when it came time to sell the house. That didn't mean that she had to buy the gravel from Connor's gravel lot. She might not get her money back if she went elsewhere, but the single pickup truck' load of marble chips hadn't cost very much, and she wasn't sure she wanted to go back there.

She was almost certain Connor was the one who had killed Audrey. She had just gotten a phone call from a murderer.

The thought made her shiver. In the back of her mind, a voice that sounded like her mother's chided her not to jump to conclusions. Flora didn't feel like she was jumping to any conclusions right now, though. It seemed blatantly obvious that Connor was the killer. Sure, he might not have a criminal history or any indications of violence in his past…

Wait. She paused in her painting, narrowing her eyes as she thought back to something else Violet had said that day she forced Flora to think about her feelings for Grady.

Hadn't Violet mentioned something about Connor's wife going missing?

Knowing she wouldn't be able to focus on anything else until she had some answers, she set the paint roller down again and slipped out of the bedroom with her phone. Amaretto was lying on the floor in the hallway, and twisted around so her belly was up as Flora walked by. She paused to stroke the cat's soft fur.

"It's been a boring week, I know," she murmured. "But look on the bright side; once I'm done with this guestroom, I'll put furniture in it and you'll have a whole other room you can play in. And if you keep doing so good with the harness, you'll be able to go outside soon too."

Amaretto kicked at her hand with her back feet and Flora withdrew from the cat's stomach, heading downstairs to where her laptop was sitting on the coffee table. She opened it and clicked on the web browser. She didn't remember Connor's last name, but all it took was a visit to the gravel lot's website to get it, then she typed *missing woman coombs warbler* into the search bar.

A few articles came up. They were a good three years old, and as she read them, a dark suspicion began to rise in her.

Heather Coombs was last seen on July 4. She is believed to still be in or near the Warbler area. If you see her, please contact...

And then the local police station number. None of the articles had much to say about her other than that she had gone missing. Connor was the one who had reported her missing, and she had never been found.

There were no later articles about a body, no obituaries for her. The case seemed to have slowly just… fizzled out.

"Odd," Flora murmured.

The internet wasn't helping her, but she knew who might know more. She picked up her phone to call Grady, then remembered he was at work today. She hesitated, then called the hardware store. If he was busy, she could always wait until he got off of work to talk to him, but she knew there was a lot of down time during the day at the hardware store, and his boss wouldn't care if he was on the store phone for some of it. She was a good customer, after all. She had become a fixture there over the past few months.

She was unsurprised when Grady was the one who answered. Mr. Brant could barely hear at the best of times, and talking to him on the phone was a nightmare.

"Brant's Hardware," Grady's familiar voice said. "How can I help you?"

"It's Flora," she said. "Are you busy?"

"I'm trying to look busy," he muttered. "It's been a slow day, and Mr. Brant keeps finding odd chores for me to do. What's up?"

"Well, first, the gravel lot called. Connor said we can go get the gravel any time. Apparently, they reopened."

"Huh," he grunted. "Sooner than I expected."

"Yeah, I wasn't expecting it this soon either. That's not all, though. I remembered something Violet said to me last week. Something about Connor's missing wife?"

"I remember hearing about that," Grady said. "I heard from Connor that she ran off with another man."

"Well, she was never found, at least not according to what I could find online. Dead or alive. When combined with what happened to Audrey…"

"Yeah," he said after a moment. "It sounds like he might have a history after all. Shouldn't that be enough for the police to arrest him? If one woman he was connected to went missing and another was found dead on his property, combined with everything you and I have already managed to figure out, they should have more than enough to bring him in. So why is he free as a bird, and reopening the gravel lot?"

"I don't know," Flora said. She hesitated. "But... I want to find out."

"You want to go get that gravel, don't you?"

"I don't want to go alone. But maybe he'll let something slip in person. Flint asked me to help, and I know there isn't much I can do, but something isn't adding up, and I want to know what it is."

"We can go tomorrow evening," Grady said. "The gravel lot is open until eight, and I get out at seven. Meet me in town, and we'll drive out there together."

"One of these days I'll find a way to thank you for everything you do for me," Flora said. "For now, just know you're the best, Grady."

CHAPTER EIGHT

Getting the gravel Friday evening before Violet and Sydney came over would be cutting things close, so she called Violet the next morning to let her know she could let herself into the house if Flora wasn't there when she arrived. She left a spare key under a rock near the shed, and sent Violet a text reminding her not to let Amaretto get outside.

She finished painting the guestroom that day, and after cleaning up, she took a moment to admire the room. It was still empty, and the floorboards still needed work, but it looked miles better than it had when she moved in. She was glad Grady had convinced her to work on the shed, but getting back to making progress on the house felt even better. She would dedicate next week to the floorboards, and then it would be time to decorate the room and she would officially have a guest bedroom.

She cleaned up a little and went grocery shopping so she would have snacks and drinks for their get-together that night, and spent some time with Amaretto, working on getting the cat used to wearing her harness until it was time to meet Grady at the hardware store. She parked in the lot around back and they got into his truck together.

"I feel like I should be trying to discourage you from going back there," Grady said as he drove toward the gravel lot. "For all we know, this guy has killed two women."

"I know," she admitted. "But we aren't going to give him a reason to be suspicious of us. I just want to get some answers. And I do need the gravel."

"Don't go anywhere alone while we're there," he said. "Promise?"

"I promise," she assured him.

He drove them north of town and turned onto the road the gravel lot was on. He had to slow down before he reached the driveway, because trucks and equipment with the name Warbler Arborist Company printed on the sides were parked along the road in front of the gravel lot. Flora remembered the argument Connor had been having with his neighbor the day they found the body, and raised her eyebrows. He must be confident he wasn't going to face charges for what happened to Audrey if he was moving ahead with clearing the trees already.

Grady maneuvered around the equipment and put on his blinker to turn into the drive, but had to brake when they saw the gates were closed and a woman was standing in front of them. No, not just standing – she had chained herself to the gates, making it impossible for the police officer who was talking to her to move her, and preventing them from opening.

On closer inspection, she wasn't just any woman. It was Lacie – Connor's neighbor.

Flora exchanged a look with Grady. This was unexpected. She had a sinking feeling she wouldn't be getting gravel *or* answers today.

Grady pulled to a stop in the drive and rolled the windows of the truck down. The officer glanced up at them and she recognized Officer Hendricks. He walked over, shading his eyes against the evening sun. When he saw Flora in the car he detoured over to the passenger window instead of the driver side.

"I should be surprised to see you here, but somehow, I'm not," he said. "I heard you're the one who made that unfortunate discovery last week. Why did you come back?"

"I still need gravel," Flora said. "And I already paid for it from this place. What's going on?"

The officer gave Grady a tight nod in greeting, then sighed and ran a hand through his hair. "It's a property dispute, or it started out that way. I'm going to have to bring Ms. Hill in on a trespassing charge, but she is refusing to hand over the key for the chains. She's padlocked herself to the gates. She's refusing to let the arborists in to clear trees. The two of you are going to have to come back at a later date, I don't think we're going to get this resolved before the gravel lot closes for the day."

Flora desperately wanted to ask him about Audrey's case, but she knew he wouldn't tell her anything. Instead, she gazed at Lacie, who looked hot, sweaty, and utterly resolved as she stood in front of the gate. She frowned as she saw Connor approaching from the office on the other side of the fence. With a nod, she directed Officer Hendricks's attention that way and he gave her a brief nod before heading back to the gate to do his job.

Grady made to put the truck into reverse, but Flora shook her head and pressed her finger to her lips. She wanted to hear this.

"I just got off my phone with my lawyer," Connor said to Lacie. "Even if the criminal charges don't stick, you're going to be facing a lawsuit for this if you don't undo these chains and get off my property right now. You're costing me business, and you're costing these poor arborists their time."

"I'm not letting you cut down trees that are on my property. It's only a matter of time until I get another surveyor out here, but if I let you do this, when they prove that I'm right about the property lines, it'll be too late. Those trees will be gone. Do you have any idea how much mature trees like that are worth? Once I prove that I am on the right side of this dispute, you'll owe me tens of thousands of dollars. You'll be the one facing a lawsuit."

"I won't be facing anything because your surveyor is going to tell you the same thing I'm telling you. Those trees are on my property."

"I don't understand why you're doing this," Lacie snapped. "You have acreage in the back you can expand into. You don't need to expand towards my property. This is harassment. I... I'm going to go to the zoning commission. I'm going to go to the newspaper. You have no right to cut down my trees."

"Both of you, please," Officer Hendricks said. "This argument isn't going to go anywhere. Connor, please let me handle this. Ms. Hill, please unlock yourself and let me escort you off the property."

"He's going to destroy my property," Lacie snapped. "Can't you, I don't know, get an injunction against the arborists doing their work?"

Officer Hendricks gave a deep sigh. "This is a civil matter, Ms. Hill. You're making it into a criminal one. You're going to face charges if you don't give this up immediately."

"She's going to face charges either way," Connor snapped. "I've had enough of this."

A horn beeped behind them and Flora turned in her seat to see another police cruiser trying to get into the drive. Grady put the truck into reverse, maneuvering back onto the road. She watched as the cruiser pulled to a stop and a female officer got out with a pair of bolt cutters. She was reluctant to leave, but she knew they couldn't stay and watch the drama unfold. The police wouldn't appreciate it, and they had no reason to be here now that they had been denied entry.

"I'm starting to think my driveway is cursed." Flora sighed as they headed back into town. On the upside, she would get home in time for Violet and Sydney's arrival. She was trying to think positively, but it was hard. "We'll have to try again next week." She frowned. "If we *are* right about Connor, Lacie had better be careful. If he really has killed two women already… she could be next."

"Hopefully, the amount of attention the two of them have already garnered from the police will keep her safe," Grady said. "He can only get away with so much before it all comes crashing down on him."

"They must have a reason to think he's innocent," Flora mused. "I just wish we knew what it was."

CHAPTER NINE

Grady took her back to the hardware store so she could grab her truck, then they drove to Flora's house. They arrived before anyone else did, so the two of them dragged the grill and camp chairs out of the shed and stacked wood near the fire pit for the fire later that evening.

Sydney was the first to arrive. He had brought supplies for burgers and s'mores, so they started cooking the burger patties while they waited for Violet. She arrived a little later than expected, and apologized as she came around the house and into the backyard.

"I didn't realize I was running so late. I got caught in a conversation with a friend of mine." She smiled, looking proud of herself. "A very enlightening conversation."

"That's a dangerous look on you," Flora said. "What did you find out? Also, what do you want on your burger?"

"Everything," Violet said. "And, I found out that your informant might not be all you think he is."

Flora gave her friend a blank look while Grady started assembling the burgers. "Last I checked, I don't have an informant. Unless you count yourself, I suppose."

"I'm talking about Flint Perry, of course," Violet said. "His last name seemed familiar when you told me about him, and I remembered that one of my regulars is a woman named Alisha Perry, so when she came in today, I asked if she was related to him, and what do you know?" She grabbed a hard cider and opened it as she spoke, sitting down in one of the camp chairs Flora and Grady had set up near the grill. "He's her brother. And I can tell you, he was *not* dating Audrey at the time of her death."

Grady froze, then slowly slid the first burger over to Violet, who took it gladly. His eyes found Flora's. He looked just as surprised and confused as she felt.

"Are you sure?" Flora asked slowly. "Because he sounded pretty certain he was dating her."

"Well, according to his sister, he and Audrey had been broken up for two weeks. He was pretty upset about it, and spent a lot of time talking with her about his relationship. Audrey's the one who broke up with him, but Alisha wasn't sure why. It sounded like Flint wasn't either. Apparently Audrey gave him that whole 'let's be friends' spiel and they were still talking, but they definitely weren't together."

"Why would he lie about that?" Grady asked.

"No idea," Violet said. "Alisha didn't say it in as many words, but she alluded to a suspicion that Flint had started harassing and maybe even stalking Audrey. So, I think if the two of you see him again, you should be careful. I have no idea if he's involved in her death or not, but what Flora said he told her and what Alisha told me don't match up."

"That's good to know," Flora said. She had no idea if she would ever even see Flint again, but before she heard this, she wouldn't have thought twice about talking to him or even inviting him into her home. She would be much more cautious now.

Violet took a bite out of her burger and Grady passed the next one to Sydney. He didn't know any of the people involved in this case, so he didn't have much to say about it – a fact he was probably glad of. He grabbed a drink of his own and sat next to Violet. The two of them chatted quietly as they ate, and Flora accepted her burger from Grady before sitting down herself.

The food was delicious, and the company was even better. It was early fall now, and the days still felt summery, though it had started getting a little cooler at night. She was looking forward to her first Kentucky winter. She was used to Chicago, which could be brutally windy and cold. The winter in Kentucky was supposed to be milder, and she was looking forward to the cooler weather after the hot summer.

After they finished their burgers, they moved the chairs over to the fire pit and started the fire. Sydney brought out his s'more supplies and they sat around roasting marshmallows as the sun began to go down.

Flora felt a pang as she realized how happy she was. Did she really want to have only one more summer like this? Maybe she *should* look into buying another house in Warbler. She could stay in the area, near her friends, and just be content with making a little less money than she would if she flipped houses in a more affluent area.

"You look pensive," Violet said to her as the guys went to get more drinks from the cooler by the grill. "What's up?"

"Just thinking about what happens next," Flora said. "I'm so much happier here than I ever expected I would be. It's getting harder and harder to think of leaving, and I've only been here for half a year. It's going to be so much more difficult in another eighteen months."

"You know we all want you to stay," Violet said. "You have a lot of friends here. Not just us – I'm sure your lovely neighbor will be sad to see you go too. Whoever moves in here next might not be as willing to chat with her five times a day."

Flora snorted. "Beth isn't that bad. She's just lonely. And she only stops by once or twice a day, sometimes not even that." She grimaced. "I can't believe I'm saying this, but I would miss her too. I do want to stay, Violet, but I'm doing all of this with the help of a loan from my aunt. I need to pay her back. And to do that, I need to sell the house. I love Warbler, don't get me wrong, but I'm a little worried about making as much profit as I need to, not only to pay her back, but to then buy the next house that I'm going to work on. People are moving away from the area, not to it. Even if I get lucky with this house, there's no telling if I will with the next one. I can't gamble my entire future on Warbler's population growing just because I like you guys so much."

"I know," Violet said, leaning over to squeeze her arm. "You'll figure it out, Flora. And you know we're all happy to help if you need it. Besides, even if you *do* end up moving all the way back to Chicago, we'll still be your friends."

"I know." She gave Violet a warm smile. "It means a lot. Thank you."

"And look on the bright side," her friend said. "Maybe your unlucky streak will break if you move away. You never found a body before coming to Warbler, did you?"

Flora had not. Not for the first time, she wondered how one little town could have so many problems.

CHAPTER TEN

She spent the morning watching videos on how to strip, sand, and refinish hardwood floors. She made a list of what she needed, which somehow morphed into a grocery list too. It was late morning by the time Flora went into town to get the supplies she needed. She stopped by the hardware store first, glad that her usual spot right in front of it was open. She said hi to Mr. Brant, who was in his customary spot behind the register, then grabbed a cart and wandered the aisles. She had found half the supplies on her list by the time Grady came in from the garden center. He waved at her and came over, looking at the goods in her cart.

"You're starting on the floors?" he asked.

"Yep. I'm a little nervous, but it will be good to learn how to do it. And I'm excited to see how nice they look when I'm done."

"You're going to do a great job," he said. "Remember to get a good respirator too. That floor stain isn't good to breathe in."

"Thanks," she said. "I'm going to put a fan in the window too, to blow the air out."

"Good idea," he said. "Let me know if you need help."

"I will," she promised. "I'm hoping doing the guest room won't take me too long. I suppose I'll do the other floors upstairs next. Well, after I remove the rest of the wallpaper and paint everything. I do *not* want to have to worry about getting paint on my newly refinished floors."

He chuckled, then looked around, as if making sure they were alone. "Are you free tonight?"

"Yeah," she said. She was free most nights – she usually stopped working on the house for the evening when she got hungry for dinner, and unless she had plans with one of her friends, she spent the rest of the evening relaxing. "What's up?"

"Do you want to go to Dave's with me?"

Dave's was one of the two bars in town. Flora had been there once, with Violet, but bars weren't usually her scene. She stared at Grady. Was he asking her on a date?

"Sure," she said after a moment. "What time?"

"Eight," he told her. "Flint stopped in earlier. He asked if I wanted to get drinks tonight. After what Violet said yesterday, I wasn't sure if I should agree, but if both of us go, it should be safe enough."

She was surprised to find that she was a little disappointed this wasn't a date, but rather an extension of their extremely amateur investigation into what had happened to Audrey. The disappointment surprised her, because normally this sort of thing was right up her alley.

"Good, I'm glad you're not meeting with him alone. I'll meet you there at eight." She smiled at him, remembering what Violet had told her about her needing to make the first move. "It's a date."

After stopping at the grocery store, she went home and got started on the floor in the guest bedroom. She had to pause occasionally to rewatch part of the instructional video she was working off of, and it didn't help that she was so distracted by the "date" this evening. It wasn't really a *date* date. She knew that, but her mind still seemed more stuck on what to wear than on the fact they were meeting someone who had definitely lied to them and had possibly done it for nefarious purposes.

She still thought Connor was the most likely culprit behind Audrey's death, but Flint's lie about dating her had shaken her certainty to the extent that she was no longer sure what she believed. Maybe tonight would bring some answers.

Dave's wasn't the sort of bar where people wore cocktail dresses. She dressed in a pair of well-fitted black jeans and one of her nicer blouses, and even then, she knew she was probably overdressed. She pulled her hair into a loose braid, touched up her makeup, slipped some boots on, and then looked at herself in the mirror.

"It's not a date," she reminded herself. "Despite what you said. Just remember that. Tonight is about Flint."

She gave her reflection a firm nod and grabbed her purse. Pausing in the living room to kiss the top of

Amaretto's head, she left the house, locking the door behind her, and got into her truck.

Dave's was on the edge of Warbler's small downtown area, and the parking lot was nearly full when she got there. She parked in the back half of the lot and walked inside, already having spotted Grady's truck.

Not for the first time, she wished he had a cell phone. It would make finding him in places like this so much easier. While the noise of loud conversation and music pressed down on her, she looked around for him. He wasn't at the bar, but soon she spotted him at a table near the back, seated across from Flint. He saw her approaching when she was halfway across the room and waved at her. She was pleased to see he had already gotten her a drink, and she slid into the seat next to him. Flint nodded at her.

"Good to see you again," he said.

"You too," she said. She wasn't sure if Grady had mentioned that she would be coming or not, but Flint didn't look surprised to see her. "How are you holding up?"

"I'm hanging in there," he said. "I asked Grady to meet me here because I found something new." He picked a folder up from the seat beside him and put it on the table. "I printed these off earlier today. They are emails between Audrey and her boss at the surveying company. I don't know all the jargon, but it looks like she found something interesting while she was surveying the property bordering the gravel lot."

"What did you find?" Flora asked, sliding the folder over and flipping it open to see printed off emails inside. Her mind immediately went to the darkest of places – had Audrey found another body? Perhaps Conner's missing wife?

"Property lines." Flint gave them a serious look. "The real property lines. It turns out Connor was right. The contested portion of the property was his, that and more. The gravel lot's property lines extend into what the neighbor thought was her property. Audrey had contacted her boss because the discrepancy was so large she wasn't sure how to proceed. She knew there would be trouble and she wanted to double check her findings with someone else."

"How do you have these?" Grady asked, flipping through the files.

"I know her email password. I was wondering if there was anything in her emails that could give me some answers, and that's when I found these."

This was... unexpected. If Audrey's findings would prove that Connor was right, then what happened to his motive for murder? She was beginning to feel that she and Grady were very, very wrong with their suspicions.

"Have either of you found anything else?" Flint asked "I drove past the gravel lot this morning and saw that it was still open. I can't believe they're letting Connor get away with it."

"We're just as in the dark as everyone else," Flora said. She hesitated, glancing at Grady, and he nodded. They both wanted to get to the bottom of Flint's lie, and this was a good, public place for it. She took a deep breath. "I am curious, though. I heard from someone else that you and Audrey broke up a couple of weeks ago. What's that all about?"

Flint froze. His expression darkened, and he took a heavy gulp of his drink before setting the glass back down with a little too much force. "We weren't broken up," he snapped. "We were on a break. It was only supposed to be temporary. That's all. It has nothing to do with what happened to her."

"Is that why you didn't tell anyone she was missing?" Grady asked.

"It's why I didn't *know* she was missing," Flint said. "Look, I wasn't trying to deceive you two. We were always going to get back together. She just needed some space. That's all. I thought she was ignoring me because she was annoyed with how much I had been trying to talk to her. I didn't know she was missing. I'm not ever going to stop feeling guilty about it."

"Had she asked you to stop contacting her?" Flora asked.

He scowled. "That's none of your business."

She exchanged another look with Grady. Flint seemed to be in denial about their breakup, and she suspected his sister was right; he must have been harassing Audrey to the point she had tried to cut off contact with him.

Flint must have seen something in their glance, because he stood up suddenly. "You think I did something to her, don't you? I can't believe it. I don't need this. I'm out of here."

He stomped away, leaving his drink behind and not looking back as he rushed out of the bar.

"Well, that went well," Flora muttered as she took a sip of her own drink.

CHAPTER ELEVEN

Grady arrived at her house bright and early Monday morning. This was their third time going to get gravel. If something prevented her from doing it this time, she was going to take the loss and just order gravel from another place. This was getting ridiculous.

Grady took the now familiar route through town to the gravel lot north of Warbler. When they arrived, the gates were open, and everything seemed to be proceeding as normal. Both Jamie and Connor were in the small office building when they walked through the door. Jamie was eating a sandwich, and Connor was dipping some fries from a fast-food place in some ketchup behind the desk.

"About time," Connor grunted when they came in. "Jamie will take you back when he's done eating."

"I'll be quick," Jamie promised.

"Don't rush on our account," Flora said. She felt bad at the thought of someone hurrying through their break just to help her get some gravel. She didn't mind waiting, or at least, normally she wouldn't. She wasn't exactly thrilled to be here with Connor, though she was less certain that he was the killer than she had been before.

"How's it going?" Grady asked Connor. Flora knew he couldn't act any differently than he normally would, or Connor might realize they no longer trusted him.

"Not great," he replied. "The arborists are refusing to touch the trees until the issue with the property lines is settled. I want to have it done by the end of fall. Lacie is costing me money and time." He crumpled his fast-food wrapper and threw it with too much force at the garbage bin. It bounced off the edge and he glowered at it. "I've got the police crawling all over the place, and I've had contractors pull out of major orders. It has *not* been a good week."

Jamie got up and threw his to-go bag away. "Well, I'm all set. Are you two ready?"

"We are," Flora said.

"If you get any more projects, Grady, I hope you'll come back here," Connor said as they walked out the door.

"You've always done me right, Connor," Grady said, raising his hand in a wave as they walked through the door. It wasn't an answer, not really, but Connor seemed to take it as one.

Jamie climbed into the backhoe and gestured for them to follow him. Flora got a feeling of déjà vu as they climbed into Grady's truck and trailed the slow-moving construction vehicle through the gravel lot. They went the opposite direction from last time, heading toward the east side of the lot. Jamie stopped in front of a huge pile of marble chips and got out of the backhoe, waving at them to back up to the gravel. Grady rolled down the windows when he approached them.

"You know the drill," Jamie said. "Stay in the vehicle until I give you the all-clear."

Flora gave him a thumbs up and watched as he climbed back into the backhoe. He started to move it, but then paused and fiddled with something. After a moment, he got back out of the vehicle.

"I'm sorry, I just got a page from Connor. He set up some motion sensing alarms at the other edge of the lot, because he thinks that neighbor of his has been coming onto the property. The alarms just went off and he wants me to go check it out."

"It's all right. We can wait," Grady said.

Jamie looked relieved. "Thanks, guys. Sorry this has all been such a mess." He hesitated, looking toward the backhoe. "I hate to ask, but would you mind giving me a ride over there? This will go a lot faster if you do. My only other options are hoofing it back to the front to grab a work truck or taking the backhoe over there, and that would take forever."

Grady and Flora exchanged a look. Flora shrugged and scooted over so she could sit in the middle seat next to Grady, her leg pressed against his.

"Hop in," Grady told Jamie. The younger man grinned and went around to the passenger side. Flora felt a little squished in between them as Grady started the truck and Jamie directed them through the lot. Flora realized they were heading back to the same spot where she had found the body. Before long, the other pile of marble chips came into view. This one had caution tape set up in a big circle around it.

"Right, don't get too close to that," Jamie mumbled. "Just let me out here, I'll walk around and make sure Lacie isn't here. If she is, I'm going to need to call the police, because Connor is going to want to press charges for trespassing."

He sounded like he was at the end of his rope with all of this, and Flora couldn't blame him. It must have been stressful, working for Connor with all of this going on.

Jamie got out of the truck and walked to the edge of the lot, pausing by the tree line to look around. Flora and Grady watched him for a moment, then Flora turned her attention to the pile of marble chips. She couldn't believe she was back here, where she and Grady had found a dead body. The marble chips had been disturbed, and she was sure the police had dug through it with whatever the law enforcement equivalent of a fine-tooth comb was. She turned her head away from it, wishing Jamie would hurry up so they could just get the gravel and she could never come back here again.

Movement past the pile of marble chips caught her eye. She frowned.

"Look, there's someone out there," she said, nudging Grady with her elbow.

He followed her gaze. "That's the woman Jamie's looking for, isn't it?" he asked. "Lacie?"

Flora nodded, not taking her eyes off the woman until she vanished in the trees. Grady looked out the window, but he couldn't call to Jamie without alerting Lacie they had seen her. After a moment, he unbuckled his seatbelt and slipped out of the truck. Flora followed him, not wanting to be left alone.

"Whoa, you scared me," Jamie said, jumping as Grady came up behind him. "What's up?"

"We saw someone in the forest that way," Grady said quietly, pointing in the direction Flora had seen Lacie.

"Thanks," Jamie said. He turned and started walking that way, looking irritated. Grady glanced at Flora, and without a word the two of them followed him. He looked back, raising his eyebrows.

"Do you really want to go alone?" Flora asked before he could ask what they were doing. "After what happened here last week?"

Jamie shook his head and gave them a grateful look. The three of them continued into the forest. They were north of the main part of the gravel lot now, no longer along the shared border with Lacie. Flora saw movement ahead of them as the other woman shoved her way deeper into the undergrowth and realized Lacie was actively avoiding them. Of course – she must have heard the pickup truck approaching.

"Hey," Jamie called out, making her jump. "We see you!"

There was silence for a second, then Lacie stepped out from behind a tree. Flora stared. She had a dog with her – a big, rusty-red colored bloodhound. The dog wagged his tail, his droopy ears and jowls reminding her of Beth's Basset hound, Sammy. The hand that wasn't holding the dog's leash gripped a shovel.

"You need to leave the property right now," Jamie said. "Connor is going to press charges. The police already warned you not to come here anymore."

"I just need ten minutes," Lacie said, gripping the dog's leash tightly. "Ten minutes, please."

"What are you doing?" Flora asked. "Why do you have a dog with you?"

"Be careful," Grady said, touching Flora's elbow. "She has a gun."

He murmured the words close to her ear, and she looked at Lacie more closely, realizing that she had a handgun strapped to her hip. She froze. The police hadn't released Audrey's cause of death yet, but death-by-bullet seemed like a plausible possibility. She remembered what Flint had told them just a couple of nights ago – Audrey had found proof that the current property lines were incorrect, but in a way that favored Connor, not Lacie.

Lacie, who had a history of trespassing onto the gravel lot, and who was desperate to prove that the trees on this part of the property were hers. Lacie, who had a gun and a shovel with her at this very moment, a shovel that could have been used to bury a body in gravel.

Flora realized they might have been very wrong about everything.

CHAPTER TWELVE

"I just need ten more minutes," Lacie repeated. "If I'm wrong, you can call the police and let them arrest me, or whatever Connor is going to insist on."

"What are you even doing back here?" Jamie asked, sounding completely done with all of this. "Last time you told me you were looking for the property border markers, but you aren't even by the property border anymore. What's the point of all of this? Can't you just let it go? Connor already has to wait for the new surveyor to come out. He can't start cutting down the trees until then. Why do you keep harassing us?"

Before she could answer, the radio on Jamie's hip made a crackling sound. He grabbed it.

"What?"

"I'm on my way down there. Did you find her?"

It was Connor's voice.

Jamie opened his mouth to respond, but Lacie waved frantically to cut him off.

"Don't. Give me a chance to explain." She looked at him desperately. "Please."

Jamie hesitated. His eyes moved from the dog to the gun she was wearing and he slowly raised the radio to his mouth. "Not yet. I'll let you know if I do."

"She'd better not be trespassing again," Connor grunted. The radio fell silent.

"Well?" Jamie snapped, impatient. "What are you doing here? Why did I just lie to my boss?"

"I'm looking for his wife," Lacie blurted out.

Flora blinked, and looked at Grady, who furrowed his brows. Either Lacie was lying, or they weren't the only ones who had been investigating Connor's past.

"I borrowed this dog from my sister, who does search and rescue. He's a cadaver dog – he finds human remains."

"The police already searched the gravel lot with their dogs," Jamie said.

"They searched the gravel lot, but did they search the forest?"

Jamie frowned. Flora thought that meant the answer was no.

"Don't you wonder why Connor is so adamant about expanding the lot in the direction of my property? When he has all of this untouched land in the back part of his property? It would be a lot easier for him to cut down a swath of trees here, instead of going through a lengthy legal battle with me."

"His wife went missing three years ago," Jamie said slowly. "She ran off with another man."

"Did she?" Lacie asked. "I knew Heather. Not well, I'll give you that, but she didn't seem like the sort of woman who would do that. I had my suspicions, but it wasn't until poor Audrey's body was found that I really started to wonder. Audrey was surveying this land, and I think she found something."

"She did," Flora said, even though she knew what she was about to say was probably a bad idea. "She found that you were wrong. Connor's property extends into yours, not the other way around."

She wanted to see Lacie's reaction. The woman looked surprised, and a little sad. "She did? I really thought this part of the property was mine. My grandparents bought this place decades ago, and then passed it on to my parents, who passed it on to me. We've been wrong about it for years." She shook her head. "But that's not what I'm talking about. I think she found Heather's body."

Flora turned the woman's words over in her head. It made sense. It made a lot of sense. But they didn't have any proof.

"You don't know any of this for sure," Jamie said, as if he was reading her mind. "How do I know you're telling the truth?"

"Why else would I be here with a bloodhound and a shovel?" Lacie asked.

It was a decent point. Grady looked thoughtful, and Flora didn't know what to say. Jamie looked torn. "Well, did the dog find anything?"

"Not yet," she said. "Are you going to let me keep looking?"

Jamie paused again, then slowly nodded. "Sure. Get the dog to do whatever it does, but Connor's coming here. You've got five minutes at most."

She nodded tightly and turned to the dog, scratching behind its ears. "Ready, Ralph? Seek."

The dog turned away from them and started pulling on its harness. Lacie followed him into the forest. The three of them followed her, watching as the dog scented the air. Flora wondered if he would be able to find anything. Heather's body had been buried for three years, if she really was here. There couldn't be much left of her by now.

Lacie walked through the forest, letting the dog pull to and fro on his leash. Flora was beginning to wish that they hadn't followed Jamie out there. Connor was going to be here soon. If he really *had* killed two women, they could be in danger. Or if they were wrong, they might be out here alone in the forest with Lacie, who had a gun and a motive. Even Jamie might be a risk. He had been the one to find Audrey's body, and even though she couldn't understand why he would reveal the body if he had killed her, she couldn't ignore the possibility that she was still missing something.

Suddenly, the dog let out a deep bark and started pulling on his harness. Lacie stumbled but managed to keep hold of the leash.

"I think he found something," she said.

Before they could all follow the dog, a car horn sounded from the direction they had come and Jamie's radio crackled to life.

"Where are you?" Connor asked. "And why did I hear a dog? Did you find her?"

Jamie looked at them with wide eyes. "What do I say?" he whispered.

"Don't say anything," Lacie snapped. "Just follow me!"

She stumbled after the dog who was pulling with all his might and letting out loud, baying barks. Flora hesitated for a second and then followed Lacie, Grady right behind her. Jamie stumbled along in the back, and whenever she glanced at him, she could see his panicked face.

The dog stopped between two trees in a slight valley and sniffed the earth deeply before lying down suddenly, his head between his paws.

"That's his signal," Lacie said. She tossed the leash to the closest person, which happened to be Flora. She gripped the leather lead in her hands, hoping desperately the dog didn't take off again, because she didn't think she could hold onto it. He was a very large dog.

The dog didn't seem inclined to move, though. Lacie hefted the shovel, then frowned down at Ralph.

"All right, I need to dig, buddy." She glanced at Flora. "Can you pull him away? He's supposed to mark right where the cadaver – the body – is, and I don't want to hurt him."

Flora heaved on the leash. "Come on, buddy," she said. "Ralph, right? Come here."

The dog ignored her. Grady's hands gripped the leash over hers and he helped her pull the dog to his feet and away from the spot he was marking. The dog whined and strained against the leash, so Flora reached down to pet his warm side.

"There is no way this is real," Jamie said. "He didn't really just find a body did he?"

"We're about to find out," Lacie said. She planted the tip of the shovel in the soil, but Flora let Grady hold the leash on his own and stepped towards her.

"Wait," she said. "Look at the dirt. It looks like it's already been disturbed. It looks like someone covered this area up with leaves. And look, there's a piece of rebar lying there. Do you think it was marking this spot?"

Lacie frowned. "Maybe. That could explain how Audrey found it. She must have been trying to see if it was a property marker."

"If this really is a crime scene, we shouldn't disturb it."

"But I need to know what's down there," Lacie said. "This could be my last chance. Without proof, Connor will get me arrested for trespassing and he'll have time to move the body."

Without further ado, she stepped on the shovel, driving it into the soil. It was loose, just like Flora had said, and the shovel slid in easily. She shoveled the first load of dirt away and drove it down again.

"Where are you, Jamie? I heard a dog baying. What's going on?" Connor's angry voice came out of the radio. Jamie looked panicked. The next moment, Flora heard Connor shout from behind them, though not over the radio, and Flora realized he must have followed the sound of Ralph's baying into the forest.

Lacie swore and started digging more quickly.

"There you are."

Flora whirled around at the sound of Connor's voice. His face was flushed red, and he was carrying a shotgun in his right hand. He frowned in confusion at her, Grady, and Jamie, but then his eyes landed on Lacie and his expression turned to one of hate.

"What are you doing?" he snapped, striding forward.

Grady handed Flora the dog's leash and hurried forward to grab Connor's arm and push him back.

"Hold on, man," he said. "You need to calm down."

Connor tried to shake him off. "Let me go. What is she doing?" He pointed at Lacie. "She can't be here."

Lacie was still digging, ignoring all of them. Flora moved a little closer to her with Ralph, worried about what was going to happen. Tension hung heavily in the air, and two of the people here had guns.

Suddenly, Lacie threw the shovel to the side and knelt down, digging through the dirt with her hands. She exhaled sharply and looked up at Flora, her eyes wide. "I found a shirt. Bones."

Morbid curiosity made Flora lean over to peer into the hole. Sure enough she saw a ragged blue blouse covering a human rib cage. She nearly dropped the dog's leash in the wave of horror that flooded through her.

"No!" Connor shouted. "Get away from there."

He whipped the butt of his shotgun into Grady's shoulder. Grady stumbled back with a grunt as Connor leveled the shotgun at them, his finger on the trigger. "You should've minded your own business," he growled. "Jamie, step back. I can't let any of these three leave."

"Whoa," Jamie said, raising his hands. "Put the gun down, boss."

"Are you with me or against me?" Connor snapped at him. "Because if you're against me, you're going to meet the same end as them."

Jamie hesitated, then slowly walked over to Connor's side. Lacie raised her hands, her face pale, and Ralph let out a low growl from his position in front of Flora.

Grady stepped back slowly until he was standing between Flora and Connor.

"You shouldn't have come back here," Connor said. "You should've stayed out of all of this."

"You killed Audrey didn't you?" Flora whispered. His eyes landed on her, but when Ralph let out a bark, he glanced down at the dog instead. She could see the gun on Lacie's hip out of the corner of her eye and took the opportunity to kick the back of Grady's leg. He twitched, but didn't look back at her, and she hoped he understood what she wanted.

"She found my wife," Connor said, biting the words out reluctantly, as if he didn't want to say what he was going to say, but needed to get the secret off his chest. "I ran in to her when she was walking back to her car. She looked shaken and she started asking me about who owned this back part of my property. I put two and two together. I was the only one here that night, and no one was around to see me kill her and hide the body. I didn't think anyone would find her, we don't use that part of the lot as much, and I've been keeping Jamie away from it more than usual. I was planning on moving her when construction on the lot's extension was finished."

"She was innocent," Grady said, drawing the man's attention. "You killed an innocent woman, Connor. What happened to you? And why did you kill your *wife*?"

"I didn't," Connor said, tightening his grip on the shotgun. "Or, I didn't *mean* to. It was an accident. I was moving some of the machinery around and I didn't realize she was standing right behind it. She had her earbuds in. She wasn't paying attention either. It wasn't my fault. I didn't even know I had hit her until I got out of the backhoe."

Flora edged a little closer to Lacie, glad when Ralph tugged forward and she could use the dog's motion as an excuse to stumble a little. Connor swung the gun back toward her and she tensed, but Grady kept talking, regaining the other man's attention.

"This isn't you, Connor. You're not a killer."

"I'm not a killer, you're right," Connor said. "I'm a survivor. I do what I need to do to protect myself." He leveled the shotgun at Grady. "Any last words?"

Lacie still had her hands up, but Connor wasn't paying any attention to them for now. Flora reached her hand out and slowly grabbed the woman's gun out of its holster. Lacie gave her a wide-eyed look. Holding the dog's leash in one hand, Flora gripped the gun in the other. She didn't know what to do. Should she shoot? She didn't think she could shoot an actual human being, not even one who was pointing a gun at them.

Then she realized Jamie was staring at her. His eyes were wide, and for a terrifying moment she thought he was going to tell Connor what she was doing.

Then he lunged forward, gripping the barrel of Connor's shotgun and shoving it up toward the sky. The gun went off with a deafening blast and Flora forced herself to ignore her ringing ears as she leveled the handgun at him. Connor struggled with Jamie for a moment before realizing he had a gun pointed at him and he froze.

"Drop your gun," Flora said, her voice shaking.

"You not going to shoot me," Connor said, sneering. "You're a woman. You don't have the guts."

"What was it you just said about being a survivor? I guarantee you I want to survive just as much as you do. So drop the gun unless you want to find out if I'll really shoot you or not."

He slowly released his grip on the shotgun. Jamie took it and stepped out of his reach. Connor backed away, realizing the tables had turned on him.

"I didn't do anything wrong," he said. "I was just protecting myself. Audrey shouldn't have been snooping back here. My wife should have been paying attention when she was around heavy equipment. I didn't do anything wrong."

"Yeah, yeah," Lacie said shakily. "Tell it to the police when they get here."

EPILOGUE

Flora hit her blinker and turned into her driveway, slowing automatically so the truck wouldn't hit the pothole too hard.

But there was no pothole. Her driveway was perfectly smooth, looking brand-new with a fresh layer of white marble chips on it. The white matched the house's white siding and the white flowers she had in the flowerbeds, and it made the yard look sharp and well put together.

Connor's gravel pit was closed and didn't show any signs of reopening now that the owner was behind bars and facing two homicide charges, plus a slew of charges for his actions towards her, Grady, Jamie, and Lacie in the forest. She had finally given in and simply ordered the gravel from a larger company, which had delivered it over the weekend.

They had even spread it out for her, which saved her a lot of sweat and hard work. She normally preferred doing things herself, but after three attempts at getting the gravel on her own, she had been glad to throw in the towel.

She grabbed her cup of coffee out of the cupholder, shut off the truck, and climbed the porch steps. She had some more cans of stain to bring in so she could refinish the rest of the hardwood floors upstairs. But those could wait. She let herself in through the front door, stooped to pet Amaretto, then made her way into the kitchen, where she put her coffee down and took her cell phone out of her back pocket. She texted Violet, even though she saw the woman only half an hour ago.

I've got news.

Her friend texted her back almost right away – it wasn't a particularly busy time at the coffee shop.

What's up? Please tell me you haven't found another body.

It's good news, Flora texted back. *I stopped at the hardware store after I got my coffee from you. I took your advice.*

I give a lot of advice. What part exactly did you follow?

I asked Grady out. To dinner. Friday night.

Violet sent back a row of exclamation marks and then, *What did he say?*

We have a date, Flora said, typing out a smiley face that she knew matched the grin on her own face.

She had never actually asked someone out before – her past partners had always been the ones to pursue her – and the feeling, while nerve-racking while she was building up the courage for it, was thrilling.

She didn't know what the future would hold for her and Grady, but she was glad Violet had convinced her to take this leap.